BLUE SPOTS

A story of hope for our aching hearts

Written by Nicoline Evans - Illustrated by Senyphine

In honor of the common bond
we find within our blue spots

Every day I walk to school,
I see adults covered in blue.

A blue spot comes when life gets rough:
the loss of family, friends, or love.

From sorrows that come with no shape
but leave a frown upon your face.

When comfort has abandoned home
upon your skin blue spots will show.

These tragic moments leave their mark
as blue spots on our minds and hearts.

I've seen folks who seem okay.
They smile as they face the day.

Others yell when nothing's wrong.
They get upset by things so small.

It seems so sad, it seems so wrong.
I never want spots of my own!
I never want to feel despair
that haunts my days like a nightmare!

On my way to school today,
something took my breath away.

A man was smiling bright and true
who was completely covered in blue!

My curiosity took the reins,
I had to ask him to explain
how a man with many spots
could live his life like he did not.

I asked, "What keeps your smile on ?
You should be saddest of them all !
You're covered head to toe in blue,
These spots have taken over you !"

"Oh dear child, you must see these blue spots of mine differently."

"I wear them proud! They set me free!
They are the reason I am me!"

" When I was young my life was tough,
for years I harbored all that stuff.
The tragic terror that I'd known
became the demons that I owned. "

"Then finally, once I grew wise,
I saw my spots as dignified.
It may sound strange, but this is why:
My spots were proof that I survived."

"I let my blue spots make me strong,
they taught me how to carry on.
I learned from them the way to be
a person who lives happily."

I was unsure, I still had fear.
"What if my spots act differently?
What happens if I can't control
the way they rest upon my soul?"

"Do not worry," Blue man said,
"Don't let the sadness rule your head.
When your first spot arrives someday
remember this advice I gave;"

"Feeling sad is quite okay.
Let the tears flow as they may,
but always know inside your brain
you need not always feel that way.

Lessons come from each blue spot
if you see through the grief they brought.
They teach you all the things you love
and give you strength to rise above."

On that day my views were changed,
my thoughts on blue spots rearranged.

I saw the good that I could find
within the blue spots I'll call mine.

About Blue Spots

Blue Spots is a story for people burdened by sadness. In the city where it takes place, emotional scars appear on the characters as blue spots. In our world, these marks are internal and invisible, but in this book they are external and displayed for all to see. They symbolize the various forms of sorrow a person might encounter during their lifetime. My intention when writing this story was to instill hope. I hope it gives those who live with sadness the courage to persevere through their darkest times.

I wrote this story with children in mind, but I believe the message it conveys covers all ages. We all experience various types of sadness in our lives. It is important to know that grieving is a critical part of the healing process, but we must never dwell there. Sometimes it's hard to remember to look for the light beyond the darkness of the moment you're living in. It's easy to get lost in it and to let the sorrow consume you in unhealthy ways. I wanted to write a story addressing this. It's always nice to have a reminder that you can turn a sad situation into a positive one with the right frame of mind. It doesn't erase the pain or suffering, but it will help you transition through the grief in a healthy manner, rather than a destructive one. It is important to keep moving forward. Positive energy breeds positive outcomes. The pieces of your life may seem broken, but it is never too late to pick them up and try again. Going through hard times shapes us into stronger, wiser, and kinder human beings. If we let the lessons they bring fill our lives with strength instead of unshakable despair, I think we'd be amazed at the transformation we would see within ourselves.

Blue Spots is the first installment in an upcoming series by Nicoline Evans addressing the wide array of emotions we experience as human beings.

Printed by Morris Publishing®
3212 East Highway 30
Kearney, NE 68847
1-800-650-7888

Blue Spots

ISBN: 978-0-692-40719-6
Printed in the United States of America.

Learn more about the Author and Illustrator !

Nicoline Evans - Author

www.nicolineevans.com

Amazon : www.amazon.com/author/nicolineevans
Facebook : www.facebook.com/nicoline.eva
Twitter : www.twitter.com/nicolineevans
Instagram : www.instagram.com/nicolinenovels

Senyphine - Illustrator

www.senyphine.com

Facebook : www.facebook.com/senyphine
Twitter : www.twitter.com/senyphine
Instagram : www.instagram.com/senyphine